F. Denison

Genealogical Records of a Section of the Burrows Family

Anatiposi

F. Denison

Genealogical Records of a Section of the Burrows Family

Reprint of the original, first published in 1872.

1st Edition 2023 | ISBN: 978-3-38214-316-9

Anatiposi Verlag is an imprint of Outlook Verlagsgesellschaft mbH.

Verlag (Publisher): Outlook Verlag GmbH, Zeilweg 44, 60439 Frankfurt, Deutschland
Vertretungsberechtigt (Authorized to represent): E. Roepke, Zeilweg 44, 60439 Frankfurt, Deutschland
Druck (Print): Books on Demand GmbH, In de Tarpen 42, 22848 Norderstedt, Deutschland

GENEALOGICAL RECORDS

—OF—

A SECTION OF THE

ARRANGED BY

REV. F. DENISON.

"Bury me not, I pray thee, in Egypt.–GEN. xlvii. 29.

1872.

INSCRIBED

TO

JOSEPH BURROWS, ESQ.,

(VII. GENERATION),

OF PROVIDENCE, R. I.

AT WHOSE INSTANCE

THE RECORD HAS BEEN PREPARED
AND PUBLISHED.

PREFACE.

——o——

THIS Record proceeds by families. The families are presented in the order of their generations, beginning with Robert Burrows, and the generations are indicated by large Roman numerals standing at the head of each family. Different families of the same generation from Robert, bear the same numerals, and may readily be traced back by the lines mentioning the parentage of each. The arrangement is on a novel plan, and has its evident advantages to families. And hereafter families may easily continue the line of the record. It is hoped that the blanks now existing in some of the first generations, through dilligent inquiry may yet be filled.

For the records of the four first generations, we are indebted to the zeal and perseverance of the late Denison Burrows (vii.), of Groton, Ct. For particulars of the later families, we are under obligations to Benjamin Burrows, Sen. (vi.), and John Burrows (vii.), of Groton, Ct., and Joseph Burrows (vii.), of Providence, R. I.

To avoid confusion in the study of the records, some historical facts are related, and names are introduced by notes, pointed out in the text proper by note marks.

Prefatory to the records, we may here appropriately mention the tradition that, in the early settlement of New England there came, with the Pilgrims, three brothers.

John Burrows.

William Burrows,

Robert Burrows,

who, being Baptists, were driven out, by religious persecution, from Manchester, England. One of these finally settled in Pennsylvania, another in New York, and the third in Connecticut.

F. DENISON.

January, 1872.

Contents.

I.

ROBERT BURROWS,

Son of
Born in
Married **MARY ( ) IRELAND,** prior to 1642 ;
Died in Groton, Ct., August, 1682.

He had Children.

SAMUEL,

Born in
Married,
Died in

JOHN,

Born in   1642 ;
Married Hannah Culver, December 14, 1670 ;
Died in Groton, February 12, 1716.

It is believed that Robert Burrows was one of
the first who removed from the vicinity of Boston,
Mass., and settled in Wethersfield, Ct. There he
married the widow, Mary ( ) Ireland, who by her

former husband—Samuel Ireland, a man of property —had two daughters, Mary and Martha.

Near 1643, Robert, associated with a few others, made a permanent settlement at Pequot—now New London, Ct. After the due organization of New London, we find a special grant of land to him, dated June 2, 1650.

On the division of the lands, vacated by the Pequots, in Groton, Robert Burrows, John Packer, and Robert Park settled on the west bank of Mystic River. Mr. Burrows' grant, dated April 3, 1651, was " a parcel of land between the west side of the river and a high mountain of rocks." The records also say, " Goodman Robert Burrows was chosen the first ferryman, to ferry horse and man across Mystic River for a groat (four pence.)

With his house lot in New London, and his estates at Poquonnoc and on the Mystic, he was, in 1664, the third gentleman in the New London settlement, in the amount of his taxable property.

Of his son Samuel we have obtained no certain information. Both Samuel and John were presented to be freemen of the colony in October, 1669.

Robert's wife, Mary, died in Groton, December, 1672. He survived her but ten years.

II.

JOHN BURROWS,

Son of Robert and Mary (see page 7.)
Born in   1642 ;
Married **HANNAH CULVER*** Dec. 14, 1670 ;
Died in Groton, Ct., Feb. 12, 1716.

---

*Hannah was the daughter of Edward Culver.

CHILDREN.

JOHN,

Born in Groton,   1671 ;
Married Lydia Hubbard, October 14, 1700 ;
Died in Groton,   1752.

MARY,

Born in Groton,
Married,
Died in

MARGARET,

Born in Groton,

SAMUEL,*

Born in Groton,

Married Mary Chester, November 21, 1706 ;

Died in

---

* Samuel had at least two children, Samuel, born January 11, 1708, and Lemuel, born January 3, 1710. Mercy was the daughter of Capt. Samuel Chester.

ROBERT,

Born in Groton,

Married,

Died in

JEREMIAH,

Born in Groton,

Married,

Died in

ISAAC,

Born in Groton,

Married,

Died in

Among the "accepted inhabitants of Groton," in 1712, we find, of these sons, John, Samuel, Robert and Jeremiah.

In 1704, John, the father, was one of the patentees of the amended charter of the New London settlement, that up to this date included Groton. Evidently he was a man of large property and honorable position.

His remains, indicated by a large granite slab marked "J. B., 74, dyed 1716," are found in the Wightman Burying Ground, by the site of the first meeting house of the Baptists. Of the 1st Baptist Church in Groton (and the first in Connecticut) he was a liberal supporter.

III.

JOHN BURROWS.

Son of John and Hannah, (see page 9).
Born in Groton,   1671
Married **LYDIA HUBBARD,** * Oct. 14, 1700 ;
Died in Groton,   1752.

---

*Lydia, born 1675, was the daughter of Hugh and Jane (Latham) Hubbard.

CHILDREN

JOHN,

Born in Groton, November 14, 1701 ;
Married Desire Packer,
Died in Groton,

LYDIA,

Born in Groton, April 19, 1703 ;
Married   Pendleton;
Died in,

MARY,*

Born in Groton, November 4, 1704 ;
Married Nathan Fish,
Died in Groton, May 11, 1732.

---

*Mary's daughter, Abigail, married Jonathan Fish.

HUBBARD,

Born in Groton, February 10, 1707.

HANNAH,

Born in Groton, Januaay 23, 1709 ;
Married Joseph Denison,
Died in

SILAS,†

Born in Groton, October 4, 1710 ;
Married Hannah Gore,
Died in Groton,   1741.

---

† His daughter, Silence, married Richard Wheeler.

ABIGAIL,

Born in Groton, July 19, 1712.
Married,   Latham,
Died in

Amos,

Born in Groton, August 6, 1714 ;
Married Mary Rathbun,
Died in Groton, 1773.

The remains of this John, with those of his wife, Lydia, are found in the old Packer Burying Ground in Groton, on the southwestern slope of Pequot Hill.

IV.

JOHN BURROWS.

Son of John and Lydia, (See page 13) ;
Born in Groton, November I4, 1701 ;
Married **DESIRE PACKER,***
Died in Groton,

---

* Desire was the daughter of Capt. James Packer.

CHILDREN,

MARY,

Born in Groton, June 17, 1732 ;
Married Samuel Aborn,
Died in   Feb. 10, 1797.

LYDIA.*

Born in Groton,
Married John Anthony Aborn,
Died in

---

*Lydia left a son, Joseph Aborn.

PHEBE.

Born in Groton,
Married William Holdredge, May 27, 1770 ;
Died in

LUCRETIA,

Born in Groton,
Married William Burrows, Nov. 19, 1767 ;
Died in

WAITY,

Born in Groton,
Married Dea. Jabez Smith,
Died in

DESIRE,

Born in Groton,
Married Joseph Elliott,
Died in

NABBY,

Born in Groton,
Married Uriah Wilbur,
Died in

JOHN,

Born in Groton,
Married Hannah Wilbur, Sept. 13, 1761 ;
Died in Groton,   1784.

NATHAN,

Born in Groton,   1744 ;

Married, { 1st, Amy Williams, June 2, 1785 ;
         { 2d, Sarah Williams,   1788 ;

Died in New York, Aug. 18, 1808.

DANIEL,

Born in Groton,

Married, { 1st, Kezia Rhodes,
         { 2d, Abigail (E.) Park,

Died in Groton, Oct. 11, 1833.

JAMES,

Born in Groton,

Died in Groton, (young).

THOMAS,

Born in Groton,

Died in Groton, (young).

Yet another son, who died young.

The mother, Desire, died in 1808—age 93. Of her, tradition fondly relates that once, seeing the great flocks of pigeons, in autumn, flying past the hill where she resided—now Clift's Hill—she seized a gun and brought down, by a single shot, more than a score. Also, during the famous cold winter of 1740–41, she slid, in a huge chopping tray, from her chamber window, eastward over the snow-filled valley and far away across the river, near to the Denison mansion.

The husband, John, was both farmer and ship-carpenter.

IV.

AMOS BURROWS,

Son of John and Lydia, (see page 15) ;
Born in Groton, Aug. 6, 1714 ;
Married **MARY RATHBUN,**
Died in   1773 ;

CHILDREN.

Amos,*

Born in
Married,
Died in

---

* Amos, a Baptist minister, removed into the State of New York.

Silas,

Born in Groton, Aug. 8, 1741 ;
Married, { 1st, Mary Smith,   1761 ;
         { 2d, Phebe (D.) (C.) Smith,
Died in Groton, Aug. 8, 1818.

Joshua.

Born in
Married Jenny Fish, March 1, 1772 ;
Died in

ELISHA,

Born in

Married, { 1st,   Fish,
         { 2d,   Fish,

Died in

PAUL,

Born in   1753 ;

Married Catharine Haley,

Died in Groton, February 28, 1834.

NATHAN,

Born in

Married Ann Smith, July 24, 1774 ;   .

Died in

JOSEPH,

Born in

Married,

Died in

ELIZABETH,

Born in .

Married Thomas Mitchell, Nov. 16, 1769 ;

Died in

ANNA,

Born in

Married, { 1st, Abel Franklin, January 5, 1769 ;
         { 2d, David Lewis,

Died in

EUNICE,

Born in

Married Solomon Tift,

Died in

The mother, Mary, died Jan. 25, 1809—age, 87 years, 11 months.

The father, Amos, was an unordained preacher ; member of the (" New Light") Separate Congregational Church at Pequonnoc, Groton

V.

MARY (BURROWS) ABORN,

Daughter of John and Desire, (see page 17);
Born in Groton, June 17, 1732 ;
Married **SAMUEL ABORN,**
Died in   Feb. 10, 1797.

CHILDREN,

MARY,
Born in   Feb. 19, 1750 ;

Died in   Aug. 1, 1751.

HENRIETTA.*
Born in   July 26, 1753 ;
Married James Whitney,
Died in   Aug. 11, 1803.

* Henrietta had ten children.

SARAH.†
Born in   Nov. 4, 1754 ;
Married Dr. Joseph Rhodes,
Died in   January 1, 1777.

† Sarah had one son.

THOMAS,

Born in   June 8, 1756 ;
    Not married ;
Died in   March 16, 1763.

LOWERY.*

Born in   April 21, 1758 ;
Married Sarah Tucker,
Died in   February 8, 1830.

* Lowery had nine children.

CYNTHIA.†

Born in   July 19, 1760 ;
Married Pierre Douville,
Died in   October 24, 1800.

† Cynthia had five children.

JOHN ANTHONY.‡

Born in   November 19, 1761 ;
Married, { Salah Rhodes,
         { Sarah Rhodes,
Died in   April 1, 1821.

‡ John A. had three children.

MARY,**

Born in   September 16, 1763 ;
Married Thomas H. Coudy,
Died in   August 6, 1823.

** Mary had seven children.

SAMUEL,*

Born in   March 20, 1765 ;

Married Hannah Tillinghast,

Died in   January 3, 1818.

* Samuel had nine children.

DESIRE BURROWS,†

Born in   March 6, 1767 ;

Married Philip Crapo,

Died in   1859.

* Desire B. had two children.

THOMAS.‡

Born in   October 19, 1768 ;

Married, { 1st, Eliza Rhodes, / 2d, Sarah Biggs,

Died in   1830.

‡ Thomas had nine children.

HENRY,

Born in   July, 25, 1770 ;

Married Abby Baker,

Died in   September 10, 1810.

BURROWS,**

Born in   October 25, 1772 ;

Married Mary Hughes,

Died in   November 28, 1835,

** Burrows had eight children.

The father, Samuel Aborn, born March 3, 1726 ; died   September 22, 1801.

V.

JOHN BURROWS,

Son of John and Desire, (see page 18).
Born in Groton, Ct.,
Married **HANNAH WILBUR,** Sept. 13, 1761 ;
Died in Groton,   1784.

CHILDREN.

MARY,

Born in Groton,
Married Nathan Miles,
Died in

PHEBE,

Born in Groton,
Married William Thornton,
Died in

LYDIA.

Born in Groton,
Married Thomas Eldredge,
Died in

HANNAH,

Born in Groton,

Married George Eldredge,

Died in

ELEANOR,

Born in Groton,

Married Zebulon Williams,

Died in

ELAM,

Born in Groton, Sept. 6, 1773 ;

Married Sarah Denison, Oct. 15, 1797 ;

Died in Groton, Jan. 8, 1840 ;

DELIGHT,

Born in Groton,

Married Daniel Deboise,

Died in

The father, John, was familiarly known as "Sergeant Burrows," as he was a regimental Orderly Sergeant in the French and Indian war. He was present at the capture of Quebec, in 1759, under Gen. Wolfe. His pocket order book and journal is carefully preserved by his grandson, John Burrows, of Groton. Ct. It contains minute and interesting records of his services at Crown Point and Ticonderoga.

His remains, with those of his wife, are found in the old Packer Burying Ground in Groton, Ct.

V.

NATHAN BURROWS,

Son of John and Desire, (see page 17).

Born in Groton,   1744 ;

Married, { 1st, **AMY WILLIAMS,** June, 2, 1765;
         { 2d, **SARAH WILLIAMS,**   1788 ;

Died, in Chenango Co., N. Y., Aug. 18, 1808.

Children of AMY, 1st wife.

JOSEPH,

Born in Groton, July 18, 1765 ;

Married, { 1st, Sarah Rice, March 30, 1788 ;
         { 2d, Henrietta Rice, Sept. 25, 1803
         { 3d, Frances Packer, Jan. 10, 1808

Died in Warwick, R. I., Nov. 28, 1850.

WAITY,

Born in Groton,

Married Latham Fitch,

Died in Groton,

GEORGE,

Born in Groton,

Married Sarah Fitch,

Died in Groton,

BETSEY,

Born in Groton,

Married Benjamin Ashby,

Died in Groton,

AMY,

Born in Groton,

Married Mason Packer,

Died in Groton,

ABIGAIL,

Born in Groton,

Married Samuel Rathbun,

Died in Groton,

JAMES,

Born in Groton,

Married Polly Brown,

Died, (perished in Christmas storm,)   1811.

NANCY,

Born in Groton,

Married Beriah Grant,

Died in Groton,

EXPERIENCE,

Born in Groton,

Married John Woodward, January 1, 1806 ;

Died in Groton,

LYDIA,

Born in Groton,

Died in Groton,

DESIRE,

Born in Groton, 1787 ;

Died in Chenango Co., N. Y., Feb. 19, 1808.

Children of SARAH, 2d wife.

BENJAMIN,

Born in Groton, October 20, 1789 ;

Married,
- 1st, Rebecca Thompson, Mar. 17, 1808;
- 2d, Lucy Perkins, Nov. 10, 1844 ;
- 3d, (Y.) Williams,
- 4th, Sarah (R.) Holdredge, Nov. 22, 1864;

Died in

JESSE,

Born in Groton, 1791 ;

Married,

Died in

NATHAN,

Born in Groton, 1793 ;

Married,

Died in

SIMEON,

Born in Groton,

Married   Elliott,

Died in

BETSEY,

Born in Groton,

Married,

Died in

EDWARD, 1st,

Born in Groton,

Died (young).

EDWARD, 2d,

Born in Stonington, June   1806 ;

Married   Elliott,

Died in

The 2d wife, Sarah, died May 1, 1820.

During the Revolution, the father, Nathan, made two trips, with ox teams, from Groton, Ct., to Boston, Mass., conveying supplies to the patriot army.

In his last days he removed to Chenango, Co., New York.

V.

REV. SILAS BURROWS,

Son of Amos and Mary, (see page 21) ;

Born in Groton, Aug. 8, 1741 ;

Married, { 1st, **MARY SMITH,**
{ 2d, **PHEBE (Denison) (C.) SMITH.**

Died in Groton, Aug. 8, 1818 ;

Children of MARY, 1st wife.

SILAS,

Born in Groton,   1765 ;

Died in Groton,   1781.

DANIEL,*

Born in Groton, Oct. 28, 1766 ;

Married Mary Avery, Dec. 16, 1787 ;

Died in Groton, Jan. 23, 1858.

---

* Daniel became a Methodist minister—had seven sons and two daughters.

ROSWELL,†

Born in Groton,   1768 ;

Married Jerusha Avery,

Died in Groton,   1837.

---

† Roswell, pastor of Second Baptist Church, in Groton ; ordained in 1806. A sketch of his life may be found in Sprague's Annals of the American Pulpit."

ENOCH,

Born in Groton,   1770 ;

Married, { 1st, Esther Denison,
          { 2d, Hope (R.) King,

Died in

JABEZ.

Born in Groton,   1772 ;

Died in

GILBERT,

Born in Groton,   1774 ;

Died in Groton,   1775.

JOSHUA,

Born in Groton,   1779 ;

Died, (lost at sea)   1809.

MARY,

Born in Groton,   1782 ;
Married Jedediah Randall,
Died in Groton, May 25, 1871.

ELIZABETH,

Born in Groton   1784 ;
Died in Groton,   1785.

Lucy,

Born in Groton,   1786 ;

Died in Groton,   1791.

Some notice of the life of Rev. Silas, may be found in "Sprague's Annals of the American Pulpit," (Baptist volume.)

He was the founder and pastor of the Second Baptist Church in Groton, Ct.

VI.

ELAM BURROWS,

Son of John and Hannah, (see page 29) ;
Born in Groton, Sept. 6, 1773 ;
Married **SARAH DENISON**, Oct. 15, 1797 ;
Died in Groton, Jan. 8, 1840.

CHILDREN.

JOHN,
Born in Groton, Oct. 28, 1798 ;
Married Roxanna Brown, Aug. 23, 1821 ;
Died in

EUNICE,
Born in Groton, March 29, 1801 ;
Married Elam Eldredge, Aug, 12, 1821 ;
Died in Groton, May 7, 1822.

DENISON,
Born in Groton, Oct. 7, 1804 ;
Died in Groton, Jan. 10, 1861.

HANNAH,
Born in Groton, June 15, 1806 ;
Died in Groton, March 21, 1832.

PHEBE,

Born in Groton, Feb. 19, 1809 ;

Married Isaac D. Miner, May 10, 1832.

Died in

SALLY,

Born in Groton, May 22, 1811 ;

Married Nathan Noyes, March 18, 1830 ;

Died in

The mother, Sarah, born in Stonington, April 9, 1778, died in Groton, Oct 13, 1835.

The remains of Elam and Sarah are now in Elm Grove Cemetery, Stonington.

In early life, Elam was a sailor ; but most of his days were devoted to farming.

VI.

JOSEPH BURROWS,

Son of Nathan and Amy, (see page 31) ;

Born in Groton, July 18, 1766 .

Married, { 1st, **Sarah Rice,** March 30, 1788 ;
2d, **Henrietta Rice,** Sept. 25, 1803 ;
3d, **Frances Packer,** Jan. 10, 1808 ;

Died in Warwick, R. I., Nov. 28, 1850.

Children of SARAH, 1st wife.

JOHN R.,

Born in Warwick, R. I., Jan. 3, 1789 ;

Married Mary Phillips, Feb. 20, 1815 ;

Died in Providence, R. I., Oct. 29. 1861.

WILLIAM,

Born in Warwick, Dec. 31, 1790 ;

Married Lydia Carey,

Died in Warwick, Nov. 9, 1848.

JOSEPH,

Born in Warwick, July 14, 1793 ;

Married, { 1st, Maria Gerauld, Oct. 15, 1815 ;
2d, Rhoda Knowlton, July 19, 1849 ;
3d, Isabella R.(H.)Sullivan, May 30,1866.

Died in

BENJAMIN,

Born in Warwick, Jan. 2d, 1796 ;
Married Hannah Arnold,
Died in

AMY,

Born in Warwick, Sept. 4, 1797 ;
Married Charles Chase,
Died in Warwick, Sept. 30, 1865.

EDWARD,

Born in Warwick, Oct. 28, 1800 ;
Married Sarah A. Gibbs, Oct. 18, 1825 ;
Died in Providence, R. I., Sept. 16, 1850.

The first wife, Sarah, born in Warwick, March 8, 1764, Died in Warwick, Jan. 3, 1803.

Child of HENRIETTA, 2d wife.

SARAH R.,

Born in Warwick, Nov. 19, 1804 ;
Married Ichabod Potter,
Died in   Nov. 30, 1847.

The 2d wife, Henrietta, born in Warwick, March 6, 1762. died in Warwick, March 31, 1807.

Children of FRANCES, 3d wife.

MARY E.,

Born in Warwick, June 29, 1809 ;
Married Latham Fitch, June 23, 1832 ;
Died in

FANNY,

Born in Warwick, July 7, 1813 ;

Married Lewis T. Hoar, Jan. 1, 1832 ;

Died in

The 3d wife, Frances, born in Groton, Ct., Oct. 9, 1769 ; died in Warren, R. I., April 24, 1868— age, 98 years, 6 months, 15 days.

As she was fourteen years of age before our country fully emerged from the Revolution, and deeply imbibed the heroic spirit of those days of noble struggle, her patriotism ever burned with a bright and steady flame. During the rebellion, while her blessings rested upon her grandchildren in arms for her country's defense, she plied her needles, with her aged hands, in knitting for the supply of the soldiers.

Joseph, during the most of his life, was laboriously and successfully devoted to his occupation as a carpenter and joiner. The proofs of his skillful building abound in the village of Pawtucket. Late in life he turned to the culture of the soil.

VI.

BENJAMIN BURROWS,

Son of Nathan and Sarah, (see page 31);

Born in Groton, Oct. 20, 1789 ;

Married,
1st, **Rebecca Thompson**, Mar. 17, 1808;
2d, **Lucy Perkins**, Nov. 10, 1844 ;
3d, **(Y.) Williams**,
4th, **Sarah (R.) Holdredge**, Nov. 22, '64;

Died in

Children of REBECCA, 1st wife.

NATHAN,

Born in Groton, July 12, 1809;

Died in New Orleans, La., June 17, 1833.

WILLIAM T.,

Born in Groton, Dec. 26, 1810 ;

Married Almira W. Smith, July 4, 1833 ;

Died in Groton, Dec. 20, 1858 ;

HANNAH,

Born in Groton, April 1, 1813 ;

Married Franklin Gallup,

Died in Groton, Jan. 1, 1843.

BENJAMIN,

Born in Groton, Feb. 6, 1815 ;

Married, { 1st, Sarah Hammond, July 25, 1838 ;
2d, Ann M. Avery, Oct. 23, 1854 ;
3d, Frances L. Denison, Mar 26, 1867 ;

Died in

CALVIN,

Born in Groton, March 22, 1817 ;

Married, { 1st, Mary A. Niles,
2d, Catherine Gates,

Died in

EDWIN S.,

Born in Groton, April 19, 1819 ;

Died (drowned) July 2, 1836.

ROSWELL S., (twin,)

Born in Groton, Dec. 2, 1820 ;

Married Clarissa Edgecomb ;

Died in Groton,

RUFUS S., (twin,)

Born in Groton, Dec. 2, 1820;

Died in Groton, (young.)

SARAH,

Born in Groton, Feb. 19, 1823 ;

Married Franklin Gallup, .

Died in

Simeon S.,

Born in Groton, July 9, 1825 ;
Married Frances_Lewis,
Died in

Mary Ann,

Born in Groton, May 2, 1827 ;
Married Geo. Washington Morgan, Feb. 18, 1849 ;
Died in Groton, April 20, 1870.

George,

Born in Groton, Feb. 17, 1829 ;

Married, { 1st, Maria Burdick,
{ 2d, Anna

Died in

Joseph W.,

Born in Groton, Feb. 3, 1831 ;
Died, (in Pacific Ocean).

The mother, Rebecca, born June 14, 1787, died in Groton, Nov. 23, 1842.

Children of LUCY, 2d wife.

Lorenzo D.,

Born in Groton, June 24, 1845 ;
Died in the army, Virginia, March 3, 1863.

Daniel L.,

Born in Groton, April 3, 1847 ;
Died in the army, Virginia, Dec. 12, 1863.

VII.

JOHN BURROWS,

Son of Elam and Sarah, (see page 39) ;
Born in Groton, Oct. 28, 1798 ;
Married **ROXANNA BROWN,** Aug. 23, 1821 ;
Died in

CHILDREN.

EUNICE ELDREDGE,

Born in Groton, April 3, 1823 ;
Married Isaac W. Denison, May 10, 1843 ;
Died in Stonington, Feb. 16, 1861.

FRANCES ELEANOR,

Born in Groton, May 23, 1825 ;
Married Horace H. Clift, Oct. 25, 1848 ;
Died in

MARY ESTHER,

Born in Groton, April 29, 1827 ;
Died in Groton June 15, 1827.

MARY ELIZABETH,

Born in Groton, July 12, 1828 ;
Married John L. Denison, May 10, 1853 ;
Died in Norwich, Ct., Jan. 16, 1860.

LYDIA ESTHER,

Born in Groton, June 20, 1831 ;
Married Daniel Morgan, Dec. 25, 1861 ;
Died in

SARAH JANE,

Born in Groton, April 15, 1834 ;
Married Samuel Buckley, Nov. 26, 1860 ;
Died in

JOHN,

Born in Groton, July 21, 1836 ;
Died in Groton, Aug. 18, 1836.

John has been a successful and honored toiler on the sea and on the land ; one of Groton's worthies.

VII.

JOHN R. BURROWS,

Son of Joseph and Sarah, (see page 41) ;
Born in Warwick, R. I., Jan. 3, 1789 ;
Married **MARY PHILLIPS**,* Feb. 20, 1815 ;
Died in Providence, R. I., Oct. 29, 1861.

_____
* Mary died in Providence, March 15, 1865.

CHILDREN.

ROBY P.,
Born in Cranston, R. I., Dec. 11, 1815 ;
Died in Cranston, R. I., Oct. 27, 1816.

HANNAH P.,
Born in Cranston, R. I., Sept. 24, 1817;
Married Gardner M. Burgess,
Died

MARY P.,
Born in Providence, R. I., May 7, 1820 ;
Married Charles G. Stafford,
Died

John R.,
Born in Providence, Feb. 28, 1822 ;
Died in Providence, May 26, 1822.

LAVINIA P.,
Born in Providence June 4, 1823 ;
Married Thomas M. Rounds,
Died   Oct- 22, 1865 ;

AMEY,
Born in Providence, July 27, 1825 ;
Died in Providence, May 5, 1826.

JOHN R.,
Born in Providence, Sept. 22, 1826 ;
Died

SMITH,
Born in Providence, May 15, 1829 ;
Married Henrietta Turner,
Died

NATHANIEL P.,
Born in Providence, Oct. 30, 1831 ;
Married Sarah Sherman,
Died

CHARLOTTE T.,
Born in Providence, April 1, 1834 ;
Died in Providence, April 30, 1835.

MARCY R.,
Born in Providence, Sept. 20, 1836 ;
Died in Providence, March 15, 1837.

MARIA,
Born in Providence Oct. 22, 1839 ;
Died in Providence, Oct; 22, 1839.

ALBERT M.,
Born in Providence, Dec. 8, 1840 ;
Died in Providence, Sept. 3, 1841.

VII.

WILLIAM BURROWS,

Son of Joseph and Sarah, (see page 41) ;
Born in Warwick, R. I., Dec. 31, 179J ;
Married **LYDIA CAREY,***
Died in Warwick, Nov. 9, 1848.

* Lydia died April 17, 1842.

CHILDREN.

WILLIAM H.,

Born in Warwick, R. I., May 24, 1810 ;
Married Clarissa W. Hillard, Aug. 6, 1839 ;
Died in Fall River, Mass. March 21, 1857.

NATHAN R.,

Born in Warwick, Jan. 25, 1812 ;
Married Nancy A. Trafford, March   1835 ;
Died in Fall River, Mass., May 15, 1863.

MERCY,†

Born in Warwick, Oct. 7, 1818 ;
Married William Batty, April 19, 1837 ;
Died

† Mercy had a daughter, Huldah E.

JAMES M.,*

Born in Warwick,   1820 ;
Married Abby Read,
Died   May 6, 1863.

* James M. had a son, James.

LYDIA,

Born   July   1829 ;
Married Charles Richards, April   1847 ;
Died

VII.

JOSEPH BURROWS,

Son of Joseph and Sarah (see page 41) ;

Born in Warwick, July 14, 1793 ;

Married, { 1st, **Maria Gerauld,** Oct. 15, 1815 ;
2d, **Rhoda Knowlton,** July 19, 1849 ;
3d, **Isabella R.(H.)Sullivan,**May 30,

Died in   [1866.

Children of MARIA, 1st wife.

CALEB G.,

Born in Providence, R. I., March 4, 1817 ;

Married, { 1st, Elizabeth Holmes, Oct. 15, 1838 ;
2d, Maria L. (S.) Gibson, Jan. 27, 1869;

Died in

HENRIETTA,

Born in Providence, Nov. 26, 1818 ;

Died in

JULIA ANN G.,

Born in Providence, April 8, 1822 ;

Married George W. Hayward, Nov. 9, 1840 ;

Died in

Maria G.,

Born in Providence, July 22, 1824 ;
Married John R. Tillinghast, Oct. 20, 1852 ;
Died in

Robey,

Born in Providence, Sept. 3, 1826 ;
Died in Providence, Dec. 19, 1827.

Almira,

Born in Providence, Sept. 11, 1828 ;
Died in Providence, March 22, 1854 ;

Joseph R.,*

Born in Providence, Nov. 21, 1830 ;
Died in Providence, Dec. 8, 1862.

---

* Joseph R., served in the 10th R. I. Regt. for the overthrow of the rebellion.

Daniel,

Born in Providence, Feb. 28, 1834 ;
Married Mary A. Davis, Nov. 14, 1861 ;
Died in

George,

Born in Providence, Oct. 30, 1836 ;
Died in Providence, July 19, 1839;

The 1st wife, Maria, born in Warwick, March 19, 1796, ; died in Providence, May 8, 1847.

The 2d wife, Rhoda, born in Woodstock, Ct., Feb. 11, 1795 ; died in Providence, Feb. 22, 1865.

The 3d wife, Isabella R. (H.), born in Scotland, March 24, 1796 ; died in

Joseph learned the carpenter's trade of his father, but early in life removed to Providence, where he has been alike prospered and honored.

To him, for sufficient reasons, this volume of records has been dedicated.

VII.

BENJAMIN BURROWS,

Son of Joseph and Sarah, (see page 41) ;
Born in Warwick, R. I., Jan. 2, 1796 ;
Married **HANNAH ARNOLD,** 1819 ;
Died in

CHILDREN.

EPHRAIM A.,
Born in Warwick, R. I., Nov. 22, 1819.

HENRY A.,
Born in Providence, R. I., March 28, 1827.

DAVID A.,
Born in Providence, April 1, 1829.

AMY ANN,
Born in Providence, Sept. 22, 1832.

BENJAMIN F.,
Born in Providence, Jan. 1, 1834.

GEORGE W.,
Born in Providence, March 5, 1839.

VII.

EDWARD BURROWS,

Son of Joseph and Sarah, (see page 41) ;
Born in Warwick, R. I., Oct. 28, 1800 ;
Married **SARAH ANN GIBBS**, Oct. 18, 1825 ;
Died in Providence, R. I., Sept. 16, 1850.

CHILDREN.

EDWARD G.,

Born in Providence, R. I., May 14, 1828 ;

Married, { 1st, Mary E. Bailey, March 17, 1850 ;
         { 2d, Sarah W. Davis, April 29, 1856 ;

Died in

ELIZA G.,

Born in Providence, Feb. 1, 1832 ;
Died in Providence, Oct. 20, 1857.

VII.

SARAH R. (Burrows) POTTER,

Daughter of Joseph and Henrietta, (see page 41);
Born in Warwick, R. I , Nov. 19, 1804 ;
Married ICHABOD POTTER,
Died in   Nov. 30, 1847 ;

CHILDREN,

SARAH F.,

Born
Died

CHARLES E.,

Born
Died

EDNER E.,

Born   Sept. 18, 1832.

LEWIS C.,

Born
Died

JOSEPH H.,

Born   Dec. 11, 1833.

EDWARD P.,

Born
Died

MARY JANE,

Born   June 3, 1835.

HENRIETTA R.,

Born
Died

JULIA A.,

Born   Dec. 9, 1846.

VII.

FANNY (BURROWS) HOAR.

Daughter of Joseph and Frances, (see page 41) ;
Born in Warwick, R. I., July 7, 1813 ;
Married **LEWIS T. HOAR,** Jan. 1, 1832 ;
Died in

CHILDREN.

ELIZA B.,

Born in   March 8, 1834.

HARRIET B.,

Born in   Dec. 21, 1836.

LEWIS T.,

Born in   Feb. 18, 1839.

FANNY B.,

Born in   March 7, 1841 ;
Died in   Feb. 7, 1863.

WILLIAM,

Born in   Feb. 10, 1843.

Mary B.,

Born in   April 6, 1845.

Joseph B.,

Born in   Nov. 21, 1848.

Charles S.,

Born in   May 27, 1856.

VIII.

WILLIAM H. BURROWS,

Son of William and Lydia, (see page 53) ;
Born in Warwick, R. I., May 24, 1810 ;
Married **Clarissa W. Hillard,** August 6, 1839 ;
Died in Fall River, Mass., March 21, 1857.

CHILDREN.

Sarah H.,

Born in   Aug. 9, 1840.

Isaac H.,

Born in   March 28, 1842.

William G.,

Born in   Oct. 11, 1843.

Amanda M.,

Born in   July 4, 1845.

George E.,

Born in   August 7, 1847 ;
Died in   April 15, 1848.

CHARLES B.,

Born in   April 12, 1849.

SOPHIA A.,

Born in   April 22, 1855.

VIII.

NATHAN R. BURROWS,

Son of William and Lydia, (see page 53).
Born in Warwick, R. I., Jan. 25, 1812 ;
Married **NANCY A. TRAFFORD,** Mar., 1835 ;
Died in Fall River, Mass., May 15, 1863.

CHILDREN.

WILLIAM H.,

Born in   July 20, 1836 ;
Died in   Mar. 18, 1841.

RUTH A.,

Born in   June 23, 1838 ;
Died in   April 5, 1844.

NATHAN R.,

Born in   Nov. 25, 1839 ;
Died in   March 28, 1841.

JULIA M.,

Born in   April 24, 1843.

WILLIAM H.,

Born in   March 29, 1844.

JAMES F.,

Born in   August 18, 1845.

SARAH A.,

Born n   July 11, 1849.

LUCINA H.,

Born in   May 7, 1853.

CHARLES F.,

Born in   Dec. 15, 1857 ;
Died in   April 8, 1861.

VIII.

CALEB G. BURROWS,

Son of Joseph and Maria, (see page 55).

Born in Providence, March 4, 1817 ;

Married, { 1st **Elizabeth Holmes,** Oct. 15, 1838;
{ 2d, **Maria L.(S.)Gibson,** Jan.27,1869;

Died in

Children of ELIZABETH, 1st wife.

GEORGE HOLMES,

Born in Providence, September 2, 1839 ;
Died in Providence, May 23, 1844.

SUSAN ABORN,

Born in Providence, December 20, 1842 ;
Married James T. Kenyon, October 15, 1863 ;
Died in

EMMA FRANCES,

Born in Providence, November 16, 1845 ;
Married Herbert W. Ladd, May 25, 1870 ;
Died in

The first wife, Elizabeth, daughter of John and Sarah (A.) Holmes, born in Providence, R. I., April 21, 1818 ; died in Providence, Jan. 7, 1867.

The Second wife, Maria L., daughter of Smith and   Steere, born in Norwich, N. Y., March 3, 1827 ; died in

VIII.

DANIEL BURROWS,

Son of Joseph and Maria, (see page 55).
Born in Providence, February 28, 1834 ;
Married **MARY A. DAVIS,** November 14, 1861;
Died in

CHILDREN.

Joseph R.,
Born in Providence, November 30, 1862 ;

Died in

Herbert L.,
Born in Providence, April 4, 1868 ;

Died in

VIII.

Julia A. G. (Burrows) Hayward,

Daughter of Joseph and Maria, (see page 55).
Born in Providence, April 8, 1822 ;
Married **George W. Hayward,** * Nov. 9, 1840;
Died in

---

* The father, George W., son of Benjamin and Phila B. Hayward, was born in Middleboro, Mass., November 23, 1817.

CHILDREN.

MARIA B.,

Born in Providence, May 6, 1842 ;
Died in Providence, August, 6, 1842.

JOSEPH B.,

Born in Providence, May 24, 1845 ;
Married Phebe H. Ralph, Mar. 29, 1871 ;
Died in

ANNIE L.,

Born in Providence, February 5, 1852 ;
Died in Providence, March 3, 1857.

GEORGE W., JR.

Born in Providence, January 1, 1858 ;

Died in

VIII.

EDWARD G. BURROWS,

Son of Edward and Sarah A., (see page 59)
Born in Providence, R. I., May 14, 1828.

Married, { 1st, **Mary E. Bailey,*** Mar. 17, 1850;
{ 2d, **Sarah W. Davis,** April 29, 1856;

Died in ———

* Mary E. died August 6, 1853.

CHILDREN.

SARAH A.,

Born in   February 12, 1857 ;
Died in   September 13, 1857;

EDWARD G.,

Born in   September 23, 1858 ;

WILLIAM E.,

Born in   August 22, 1860 ;

ANNA C. C.,

Born in   July 18, 1864;

CHARLES D.,

Born in   January 19, 1867 ;

HARRIET E.,

Born in   September 26, 1871;

NOTE.

The blank places left in these Records—some belonging to the dead, and some to the living—that we are now obliged to leave, may be filled with pencil hereafter as further information shall be obtained, and as changes shall occur to the living.

Be it remembered, the Record now terminates with the close of 1871.　　　　　　F. D.